The Necronomicrap: A Guide To Your Horooooscope

by Tim Frayser
"America's Most Trusted Astrologer"

ISBN: 978-1-945941-33-7

Second Edition is the first perfect-bound edition
First Edition was saddle-bound
Copyright © December, 2002 by Tim Frayser

Yard Dog Press
710 W. Redbud Lane
Alma, AR 72921-7247

http://www.yarddogpress.com

Edited by Selina Rosen
Technical Editor Lynn Stranathan
Cover art by Mike Cole

Printed in the United States of America
0 9 8 7 6 5 4 3 2

Dedication

To my family and friends,
who put up with me,
and to Donna,
for whom the Sun shines.

Table of Contents

The Art of Astrooology

From the dawn of time, mankind has looked up at the stars and thought, "I'm hungry!" A little while later, mankind looked up at the stars and thought, "Hey, lookit those thingys up there! I wonder if I can eat them..?"

Soon, after getting some supper, mankind started watching the lights in the sky, and noticed that some of the lights moved in patterns. The lights that didn't move obviously had poor agents. People that recognized the patterns of the lights got so they could predict what they were going to do next. It got to a point where the Number Two caveman in the cave told everybody, "Okay, if the gods think the Number One caveman should be replaced by me, THAT light THERE will move THAT WAY tomorrow night..." As the fires of the cave lit up the following night to celebrate the inauguration of a new Number One caveman — and the barbecuing of the former Number One caveman — the art of Astrology was born.

Now, skeptics might argue that the picture of your prom date you keep hidden from your spouse deep in your wallet has much more of an effect on your everyday life than an astrological body millions and billions of miles away. This is UNTRUE. Astrology is REAL, as real as any space borne missile defense system could ever be. Questioning the veracity of astrology makes you a "skeptic," and, of course, nobody wants to be one of them. I mean, it's okay to question why 25 cent boxes of macaroni and cheese are "on sale" three for a dollar, but questioning astrology is just not done.

Tim Frayser

Planets, Asteroids, Moons, Stars, Hearts, Clovers:
The Things Far Away
That Make You Do What You Do

On the day you were born, indeed the very moment you emerged into the real world, your personality, character and entire future were branded onto your soul like a bad credit rating. This is done by the power of the planets, and when the light from these astrological bodies shines on you for the first time, their powers influence what happens to you for your whole life. Got it? It doesn't matter if you're way inside a hospital, or deep inside a cave, away from any outside light until days after you're born, whatever happens to be above the horizon at the moment you're born makes the template for your life. That's pretty much it. Remember: if it's an object in space, it has some kind of effect on your life.

End of story.

Tim Frayser

The Influences of the Planets

Objects in the sky don't just influence you they also influence each other, which really throws a wrench in the works. How the planetary objects deal with each other affects how their energies influence you. It can get tricky. Some of the planets cancel each other out, some planets change the influence of others, and some work together to create an entirely different kind of influence. It would be too complicated to explain every little influence in detail. The important thing is to believe whatever your astrologer tells you, and to pay cash in advance.

The Sun   Okay, so the Sun isn't exactly a "planet," but what are you gonna do? The Sun makes things brighter. Well, duh. It rules over hope, courage, and sunburns. The planets, moons and other objects in the solar system all revolve around the Sun, and frequently ask its opinion on matters of the day.

Mercury   Influences fast things, like sports cars and streakers. It is neutral and hot, and makes you sweat in embarrassing places. Mercury's cratered surface resembles Earth's Moon, and they often get confused for each other at parties.

Venus   Governs the feminine aspects of a personality, responsible for art, emotions, and feeling really cranky three days out of the month. It knows the answer to what's love got to do with it. Venus tends to tell the best jokes.

The Moon   (Okay, the Moon isn't a planet, either. Get off my back.) Influences romantic feelings in women and harvesting feelings in farmers. The Moon makes you feel hungry halfway into the movie. When full, it makes some people hairier than usual.

Mars   Controls the masculine aspects of a personality, such as drinking beer and killing things. The presence of Mars signifies strength, action, hard work and popular sporting events. It grunts a lot.

Jupiter   The biggest planet, and pretty darn smug about it, too. Jupiter controls feelings of pride and eating. If you're proud of what you can put in your mouth, thank Jupiter. Jupiter prefers creature comforts and tends to aim for the big lounge chair in the evenings.

Saturn   Saturn is a big, gassy planet, and if it wasn't for the bright, pretty rings around it, Saturn would be a lot more gassy. Saturn is the planet that influences structure, organization, and how well you are at playing "Twister."

Uranus   (Original name: Urbutt.) Uranus is a positive, rash, sneaky planet, the kind of planet that might re-wrap last year's birthday present and give it back to you next year. It harbors rebellion, encourages revolution, and likes to stick it to The Man.

Neptune   Neutral and neurotic, that's Neptune all over. It governs secrecy, spiritual idealism, and bowel movements. It likes to write letters to death row inmates. Neptune has a negative influence on today's youth.

Pluto   The planet farthest from the Earth, and therefore the one with the least influence. Accordingly, Pluto governs feeling of apathy, because it could frankly care less. It also influences the unconscious mind and other stuff you wouldn't understand.

~~~~~~~~

The moons of each of these planets, as objects in space, also influence the lives of people on Earth. Astrologers who do not take these into consideration aren't as smart as they say they are, so there. Mercury and Venus have no moons, and as a result are both in intense therapy trying to cope.

Martian Moons:

Phobos   Responsible for making you afraid of moons.

Deimos   Influences which detergent you feel like buying.

Jupiter Moons *(Note: the moons of Jupiter are called Jovian moons because they're so happy.):*

Metis, **Adrastea**, **Amalthea** and **Thebe**   Highly-unionized Jovian moons, constantly pressuring the other moons to petition for better wages.

Io   A big, ugly moon that governs your feelings towards politicians. Particularly, big, ugly politicians.

Europa   Influences the spread of grout in bathroom tiles.

Ganymede   Governs the amount of fizz shaken-up pop bottles contain.

Callisto   Nobody knows what the hell Callisto does, and most astrologers agree it's just there for looks.

Leda, **Himalia**, **Lysithea**, **Elara**, **Ananke**, **Carme**, **Pasiphae** and **Sinope**   May influence if not regulate economic confidence in a pre-wartime society.

The Moons of Saturn regulate various aspects of human flatulence:

Pan and **Atlas**   Volume.

Prometheus and **Pandora**   Range.

Epimetheus   Timbre.

Janus   Oscillation.

Mimas   Duration.

Enceladus   Meter.

Tethys, **Telesto** and **Calypso**   Tone.

Dione and **Helene**   Rhythm.

Rhea   Ripeness.

Titan   Viscosity.

Hyperion   Tempo.

Iapetus   Intensity.

Phoebe   Resonance.

Uranus Moons:

Cordelia, **Ophelia**, **Bianca**, **Cressida**, **Desdemona**, **Juliet**, **Portia**, **Rosalind**, **Belinda** and **Puck**   Collectively, these moons control how wet you get when you run in the rain.

The remaining moons of Uranus (*Miranda*, *Ariel*, *Umbriel*, *Titania*, *Oberon*, *Caliban*, *Sycorax*, *Prospero*, *Setebos*, and *Stephano*) all join together to influence the quality of TV reruns.

Neptune Moons:

Naiad, *Thalassa*, *Despina* and *Galatea*   Moons that govern the growth of crops in areas of fluctuating carbon dioxide levels.

Larissa   Influences how well you can fake it.

Proteus   The name of that little submarine in "Fantastic Voyage," and the moon that controls road rage.

Triton   You know how you're walking down the street and come face to face with someone so you step to one side to get out of their way but they step the same direction to get out of your way so you step the other way at the same time they step the other way so that the two of you are doing a little dance together on the sidewalk? Triton governs that.

Nereid   The moon that controls Ruthenium, a hard, white metal, number 44 on the periodic table of elements, which oxidizes in air at about 800 C.

Pluto Moons: Pluto has one moon, *Charon*, which influences the accumulation of navel lint.

Asteroids are large rocks that mostly orbit the Sun from within the Asteroid Belt, cruising the highways and byways between the orbits of Mars and Jupiter. Some Asteroids, such as Ceres and Vesta, are considered "minor planets," and as such are almost big enough to go to the store by themselves. As objects in space, they contribute a small yet significant influence to astrological calculations. Their contribution is to act as static. Asteroids interrupt the influential planetary signals from space in much the same way going through a tunnel interrupts radio signals, usually when your favorite song is on. The horoscopes in this book have taken the asteroid static into consideration, and compensations have been made to the relatives of the victims.

Comets are what happen when the universe goes, "Whoopsee!" They like to hang out in the Oort Cloud, outside the solar system, where the reception is much better, but sometimes go for a joyride into the inner

Solar System. Comets are a wild card in the whole astrology game, and their appearance can mean anything from global disaster to the cancellation of your favorite comic strip. It can be a tough call.

Tim Frayser

When the Planetary Influences Don't Work

Sometimes, horoscopes don't always accurately predict what's going to happen. Sometimes they miss the mark. Sometimes, they are even just plain wrong. This doesn't mean astrology doesn't work, because it does. Astrologers are always right, even when what they write is wrong. This is because of Free Will. Free Will is the basic human desire to do whatever the heck it wants to do, no matter what the astrologers (who are never wrong) say they are going to do. Free Will is a bad thing, and should be suppressed whenever possible.

Tim Frayser

The Signs of the Zooodiac

**Aries: (March 21 — April 19)

The sign of the Ram, the truck of the Dodge, is often adventurous to the point of being a real bozo. In personal relationships Aries tends to be passionate but sloppy. The ruling planet is Mars, and the ruling candy bar is Snickers.

Likes: Walks in the moonlight, Muppets.

Dislikes: Chewing tobacco, Scooby-Doo cartoons.

**Taurus: (April 20 — May 20)

The Taurus personality is patient and persistent, so they make really good snipers. They are sexually experimental, but worry someone might see them wearing silly hats. The birth stone is Emerald, and the capital of Delaware is Dover.

Likes: Ramen noodles, giant Japanese robots, beer.

Dislikes: The song "Feelings", dill pickles.

**Gemini: (May 21 — June 21)

The sign of the Twins likes to double up on everything, making them unwelcome at buffet dinners. They are intellectual and can be pretty darn snooty about it. The color for Gemini is green, not blue-green or forest green but more of a lime green.

Likes: Early-morning cuddling, shiny objects, puns.

Dislikes: Pain, humiliation.

**Cancer: (June 22 — July 22)

The sign of the Crab has a long memory for people who have borrowed books and not returned them. They dislike being told what to do, even when they are on fire. Their ruling planet is the Moon, which is 384,800 kilometers away.

Likes: Baseball caps, Beatles music.

Dislikes: Early check-outs, people that never write when they said they would.

**Leo: (July 23 — August 22)

The sign of the Lion has a natural fondness for Signourney Weaver movies. Leos are spontaneously warm hearted right up to the point where they rip out your throat and drag your carcass back into the high grass. Their ruling planet is the Sun, which isn't really a planet at all but a star, if you want to be technical about it.
Likes: Star Trek, onion rings, cold beer.
Dislikes: People who change lanes without signaling, reruns.

**Virgo: (August 23 — September 22)

Virgo is the sign of the Virginian: people born between noon and 4 PM are technically West Virginians. Virgos have charm and dignity, and like to do it standing up. The birth stone is the sardonyx, which nobody has ever heard of.
Likes: Chocolate pudding, the space program, Godzilla movies.
Dislikes: Cleaning the kitty box, twangy country music.

**Libra: (September 23 — October 23)

The sign of the Scales likes to keep things fair and even, but still manages to hog the covers. The Libra character is sensitive and artistic, so they tend to get beat up a lot in biker bars. The ruling planet is Venus and the soup of the day is chicken noodle.
Likes: Television weather ladies, celery, Doc Savage novels.
Dislikes: Lawsuits, t-shirts that shrink after one wash.

**Scorpio: (October 24 — November 21)

The sign of the Scorpions also likes Bon Jovi and Ozzy Osborne. They have strong, intense feelings toward intimate partners and anyone wearing leather chaps. Their birth stone is opal and their cars are Chevys.
Likes: Martial arts, good books, ice cold beer.
Dislikes: High places, dry counties.

**Sagittarius: (November 22 — December 21)

The sign of the Archer likes to watch slow-motion movies of women on trampolines. Sincere and honest in love, they usually have "inny" belly buttons. Their color is purple, and they prefer boxers instead of briefs.

Likes: E-mail from friends, cheesecake.
Dislikes: Math, war.

**Capricorn: (December 22 — January 19)

Unlike most of the people they hang out with, Capricorns usually have a job. Their color is brown, as if they had any say in it. In personal relationships, they pretty much give it away.

Likes: Saturday morning cartoons, writing, late-night bull sessions.
Dislikes: The icky stuff at the bottom of a can of Spam, hypocrites.

**Aquarius: (January 20 — February 18)

The sign of the water retainer is really moody at least once a month. Aquarians like music and are really good at changing flat tires. They tend to leave the toilet seat up.

Likes: Dr. Pepper, warm windy nights, spaghetti.
Dislikes: Extended-cab pickups, Steven Segal movies

**Pisces: (February 19 — March 20)

Pisces is the sign of the Fish, traditionally a trout. They like to play Neil Sedaka music in the bedroom. Their planet is Neptune, and their insurance is term life.

Likes: Soaking in a hot tub, telling jokes.
Dislikes: Long commercial breaks, the word "rural".

Tim Frayser

The Elemental Tricycles
(cue dramatic music)

The twelve signs of the Zooodiac can be further compartmentalized and segregated into elemental signs, for the simple reason that a person can never have too many labels. Each of the signs reflect the qualities of one of the four original elements: Fire, Earth, Air and Water. The periodic table was at one time very easy to remember. The elements divide the signs into four tricycles of three signs each:

Fire (Down Below) Signs: Aries, Leo, Sagittarius.
Earth (Final Conflict) Signs: Taurus, Virgo, Capricorn.
Air (Ball) Signs: Gemini, Libra, Aquarius.
Water (Balloon) Signs: Cancer, Scorpio, Pisces.

The tricycles describe character through their links as well as their weakest links to the elemental components of nature expounded by the ancient secret mystic masters, the ones who carried candles and wore those cool hoods.

The Fire signs are active, self-adhesive, creative, energetic and impatient while standing in line. They like to dance on tables during happy hour. At football games, they watch the cheerleaders.

The Earth signs are practical and reliable, like a Dodge Caravan, the most popular SUV on the market. Earth sign people are the kind of people you get to co-sign for a loan. They always have an extra key, and bug you about wearing your mittens.

The Air signs are intelligent, insolvent, sociable, and like to take long walks on the beach with a metal detector. They can fart on cue. An Air sign person always has lots to say, unfortunately.

The Water signs are over-emotional, institutional, poetic and make stuff up a lot. In matters of love, they like to keep whipped cream handy. They usually file their taxes on time and can drink like fish.

As for compatibility, it is widely known by panels of experts everywhere that Fire signs should stick together in the same bowling leagues, or hook up with Air signs. Water signs should hang together in their hoods, or invite Earth signs into their cribs. Air and Earth signs get along well during the holidays. Fire signs put out Water signs, scissors cut paper, and paper covers rock. Certain segments of the element tricycles have been copyrighted by the singing group Earth, Wind & Fire, so consult your lawyer before doing anything.

Anything at all.

Your Yearly Astrooological Forecasts

January

~ Aries
Your personal income, resources and values are in the spotlight this month, but try to take the investigations in stride. The detectives are only doing their job. Have fun with the wire taps by singing karioke with all your favorite music – talk about a captive audience!

~ Taurus
Pleasure is heading your way. Hidden desires will explode in waves of intense excitement. Who would have thought you'd get so much fun from pictures in a magazine? Your lucky numbers this month are all but the number 4.

~ Gemini
An extended trip may be in your immediate future. An adventure awaits! Pack a bag and be ready to leave town for about 6 to 8 months, depending on how the sentencing judge is feeling.

~ Cancer
Turn on the fan before you leave the bathroom Woo! Your living partner is beginning to suspect where all the money goes every month. You don't have to say a thing! You're entitled to a little fun at the race track every now and then or after work every day or all the time.

~ Leo
Maintain a dignified, stoic composure, especially when posing for photographs. Keep a serious expression on your face. That way, you won't look like an idiot when they flash your picture on the evening TV news.

~ Virgo
You will feel like an unstoppable goddess of love which, if you're a guy, you may or may not be completely comfortable with. This will be

the month you finally answer the question: How many live frogs can I fit inside my pants? Repeat this month's affirmation: I will use the turn signals when changing lanes.

~ Libra
Feel the anticipation of the new year. There is harmony relating to your personal finances as long as lines of communication remain open with your bookie. It's amazing what a little lubricant in the right place can do for your whole outlook on life. Pluto is in opposition to higher taxes.

~ Scorpio
Interpersonal relationships remain difficult. Life can be tricky sometimes. This month, you will be spending a lot of time around your home, at least until that electronic bracelet comes off your ankle. Try to finish one before opening the next.

~ Sagittarius
Get ready to be dumped big time by someone you really care about. That way, if it doesn't get around to happening this month, you'll be prepared when it finally does happen. This is, after all, you we're talking about.

~ Capricorn
Buy two pagers and set both of them on "vibrate." Then, keep one in each of your breast pockets of your shirt. That way, if you ever have a heart attack, you'll be able to use your cellphone to defibulate yourself.

~ Aquarius
Expand your horizons. Explore new sights. Allow yourself to dream. There really is life beyond the all-you-can-eat buffet table. Remember: the moist towelette is your friend.

~ Pisces
You are on a roll, although you probably would have preferred a danish. Your metaphysical spirituality will be challenged by all the negative aromatherapy downwind from the pig farm. Someone you thought you knew but didn't really know that well will say something to someone you don't know at all and never will.

February

~ Aries
You seem to be putting a lot of time and effort into something that not only isn't giving anything back to you, it doesn't even purr. It may even bite you when you're not looking. Keep out of its way when it's eating.

~ Taurus
Between the 3rd and the 10th, you will have the urge to discuss your deepest feelings with everyone, but it will start to get old by the 7th, and by the 9th your friends will stop taking your phone calls. Be sure to pay your electric bill by the 15th to avoid any service cutoffs.

~ Gemini
Events will occur this month to challenge your lifestyle, your beliefs, and your secret obsession with pink lace fringe. Avoid any TV shows that feature people making animal noises. Repeat this month's affirmation: I will work at loving myself more and keeping a towel handy for when I do.

~ Cancer
The movements of the planet Saturn will have you wondering why you can't ever find the mayonnaise when you really want it. You'll begin to see the inner beauty of people, and not just their flaws and prejudices and hypocrisy and shallow personalities and seething
resentment for their mind-numbing jobs. Watch what you lick.

~ Leo
Advances will be made in a long-term relationship, but not by you. You'll just sit on your butt like you always do, while everyone else does all the work. Love, like the Panama Canal, is a two-way street.

~ Virgo
You will meet someone who is very comfortable their personal body image, unfortunately. Look to others for help when you need to jump start your battery. Liberate the beer gut of your dreams from the repressive tight trousers of everyday life.

~ Libra
Forces are at work which will create challenges for you this month. The reason for this conjunction of events is unexpected: Neptune, Uranus and Jupiter have a thing going. Expect personal relationships to expand in strange and unexpected ways, meaning you really should've exchanged phone numbers at that one convention room party.

~ Scorpio
The person you spend intimate moments with would appreciate it if you'd stop yawning. You will learn secrets, perhaps more than you care to know, and certainly more than mere mortals should ever discover in their lifetimes, if they value their sanity. The essence of peace smells like fresh-baked bread.

~ Sagittarius
Let yourself explore different ways to tell your loved one how you feel. Your partner may explain different uses for a spatula. Use sights, sounds, and tastes, but don't confuse the whipped cream with the sour cream.

~ Capricorn
You may find people demanding more out of you than usual; a full day's work, for instance. Look for ways to compare your coworkers' faces with those of barnyard animals. It won't be long before the revolution. The next time you have your chakras aligned, take the opportunity to have them balanced and rotated as well.

~ Aquarius
A very difficult situation will resolve itself, without you having to do anything... Actually, if you do something, the situation will still be resolved, but differently. In a different kind of resolution. Of the situation. Yeah.

~ Pisces
Share a personal secret with a close friend, just to see how much of a blabbermouth they really are. Remember that dreams can actually come true sometimes, even dreams about that special person down in Accounting. Eat more peaches. In intimate matters, let your partner know just how you feel about gelatin products.

March

~ Aries
You can tell a lot about a person by whether he leaves the action figure inside the package to display, or if he takes the action figure out of the package and plays with it. Remember: you can't make an omelette without breaking a few eggs on a preheated frying pan for 2
and a half minutes with a finely chopped onion, a dash of grated cheese, some diced mushrooms, and salt to taste.

~ Taurus
You will be blind-sided by a disaster any competent system for predicting the future should have seen coming a mile away. The slow pace of events will make you think you're in a time warp, but it will turn out to just be Utah. Further investigation will require out-patient surgery by a competent physician.

~ Gemini
Worries at home will cause worries at your workplace, especially when "you-know-who" shows up drunk as a skunk. You can handle the situation. Try to laugh it off, and keep your taser handy as you notify the authorities.

~ Cancer
Don't let your Yin write a check your Yang can't cash. The planets converge on the 8th to give you special powers of sensitivity, even though you would have preferred something cool like X-ray vision or something. Try to make the best of it.

~ Leo
Jupiter needs to get out more. Stay clear of people who are unpredictably emotional, because they trigger an uncontrollable autonomic response within you. Try to perspire less. Carry a roll of paper towels with you, just in case.

~ Virgo
This month marks a new chapter in your life, although hopefully not a short, violent chapter. In matters of intimate love, try to include someone besides yourself for a change. A moment of personal humiliation will brighten the day for everyone around you.

~ Libra
Concentrate on maintaining a positive relationship with your book club. If you don't want a particular book, fill out the little slip and send it back, and if they send the book anyway, just pay for it. Don't make trouble. That special person in your life continues to wear that "I'm with stupid!" t-shirt.

~ Scorpio
The stars are forming a pattern in the midnight sky, though not one that would actually become anything recognizable, but if they did, it would really be cool. You are not nearly as hard on yourself as others would like you to be. Repeat this month's affirmation: I know that everything that happens for my higher good and is captured on the hidden video.

~ Sagittarius
Personal possessions and values will be on the agenda this month, and, in your case, for sale to the highest bidder. Get a good price. Who needs a conscience, anyway? The stars say your broken heart will heal in time, but they aren't making any promises about that femur.

~ Capricorn
A lucky break may be coming your way from an unusual source. Expect to receive some very positive news from the warden. In the meantime, be careful not to drop any soap in the shower. Everyone is amazed at how much you don't know.

~ Aquarius
You are getting very vague news in reference to your goals and career from a source that has not always been reliable and has, in the past, actually steered you in the wrong direction, causing multiple problems, but that was probably because you didn't believe enough in the power of that source's words. Heed its message, and buy another copy of this book while you're at it.

~ Pisces
You are a free-spirited individual soul, eager to discuss the great questions of existence and the meaning of life with anyone willing to buy you another beer. Finding love is possible late in the month, after your welfare runs out and you have to sell some plasma.

April

~ Aries
Cab drivers avoid you. About mid-month, you will reach that personal goal of drinking an entire gallon of milk within one hour without throwing up. Almost. If you and your partner get into an argument, have a close friend mediate so that he can give your side of the story when the authorities arrive.

~ Taurus
Spend some time interpreting your dreams, like that one with you and the twelve supermodels in the hot tub full of pudding. Okay, maybe that dream doesn't need a lot of interpretation. Go back and pick a tough one. Someone will say something to you this week that will remind you of something someone else said to you at some point in the past.

~ Gemini
You will start to wonder that maybe Moby Dick wasn't the overbearing paternal figure you'd always thought he was, but rather a symbol of the impersonal and sometimes cruel world of mid-19th century urban society. Look for a happy median somewhere along the turnpike.

~ Cancer
It's a time for reevaluation. Learn from past experiences, and think about why most people don't bonk themselves on the head with a brick on a regular basis. You'll be glad you did! Share your wisdom with a friend who seems to need it, preferably one who doesn't know the difference between your opinion and "wisdom."

~ Leo
Don't allow anyone to get close to you. Keep your distance from crowds, and avoid even answering the phone. Wear aluminum foil under your clothes to prevent radiation from getting through. Repeat this month's affirmation: With each breath, I take in light, emotions and an unknown quantity of hydro fluorocarbons.

~ Virgo
It will shock you to discover your hidden psychic spiritual animal is a banana slug. You may feel yourself drawn into an uncomfortable

situation involving leather harnesses, lemonade and goats. Use your powers of persuasion to excuse yourself, and then run like hell.

~ Libra
The passage of seasons reminds you of the inevitable passage of time, where all things pass into dust and forgotten history, reinforcing the feeling that life is ultimately futile nothing lasts forever. Try to ignore these feelings as you send off your mortgage payments. While writing your autobiography, it won't do any good to change the names
to protect the innocent, since you don't know any innocent people.

~ Scorpio
You've got a lot on your plate, so start with the mashed potatoes. While traveling, don't worry about fastening your seat belt. Nothing bad will happen to you. If anything bad happens, it'll happen to ...The Other Guy. That's right. Go right ahead. It'll be fine.

~ Sagittarius
Fight your preoccupation with the Internet, and don't let it blind you to the tremendously positive emotional benefits that come with personally interacting with real live human beings. This could be the start of something big for you.

~ Capricorn
Clear thinking this month will pave the way for important decisions, so stay off the hooch. You'll need your wits about you, and it's difficult to make rational decisions when you're hugging a commode calling for Ralph. It turns out you don't actually have as many friends as you think, since one of them is a master of disguise.

~ Aquarius
You are a special person. Don't wait for someone to put you on a pedestal climb up there yourself for when that special someone arrives in your life. Leave the sniper rifle behind this time. The Moon in its current configuration is a good sign, but not as good as the sign that says "Free Beer!"

~ Pisces
It's okay to change your mind when it comes to commitment. If a relationship is not working for you, it's time to get a big, scary dog,

change the locks and have the phone company reroute all your calls. Your belief in the power of your personal energy-channeling crystals will be shaken when you discover they're really Folger's coffee crystals.

May

~ Aries
As you enter the month of May, Mercury enters a new sign, heralding a period of extended reruns and reality-based TV shows. Cable doesn't offer much in the way of a different lineup. Luckily, you don't care.

~ Taurus
With Venus in your configuration, it's time for attracting that special someone in your life, the one that actually remembered your name. Maintaining your belief that the body will repair itself and recover spontaneously from illness if it is in a healthy environment, go ahead and cancel your dental insurance.

~ Gemini
The big, worldly issues of life, death, and the meaning of existence itself will become astonishing clear for a brief moment this month when you take just a little too long to cross a busy intersection. Plan ahead. Focus your energies on not focusing your energies so much.

~ Cancer
Hey, if it makes your partner feel good, go ahead and swallow. Neptune moves below the horizon until it's darn good and ready to come back out. You will ask yourself why a real psychic, someone who could accurately predict events in the future, would answer questions over the phone for $3.99 a minute instead of playing the lottery.

~ Leo
Jupiter in the Water sign of Cancer puts you in the mood for some down-home cookin', like the kind you're find at Pappy's Rib-o-Rama, home of the bottomless bowl of cole slaw. If you ask your friends, they will say they like you.

~ Virgo

Give your heart a chance to express itself, perhaps with an original little one-act play. Physical issues are resolved, and you may actually find yourself touching things without first drowning them in disinfectant. Learn to like jazz.

~ Libra

Don't assume the person you're interested in is a mind reader, because if that was the case, they'd know all about your little fantasy with the goats. Express your feelings. Read more comic strips. Repeat this month's affirmation: I attract wondrous opportunities and fruit flies.

~ Scorpio

Living your life to the fullest isn't something that just happens; you make it happen with sound financial planning from a certified public accountant. Stop your excuses, get out the silly hats, and have some fun. Keeping a secret this month will be difficult, especially if someone tells you.

~ Sagittarius

This month you will have a great desire to look your best and put on nice clothes and go out to dance the night away. Be careful not to let little things like eating and sleeping keep you from having a good time. You're stronger than that!

~ Capricorn

There's only one way you can make a promise to deliver something that is completely out of your control. It's called lying. Remember: some things only get better with practice. Don't just fear what you don't understand; petition Congress to outlaw it!

~ Aquarius

Love is in the air. Someone looking for romance will find their way to your door by the 19th, but you'll need at least two negative blood tests before starting anything serious. In the meantime, wear lots of plastic. Invisible lizards from the Orion Nebula will try to attack you at night, and your only defense will be to climb under the covers and hold them at bay with a flashlight.

~ Pisces

Rotate your tires. Focus on internal harmony, spiritual enlightenment, and figuring out how to program your VCR. Fluff up the pillow of your life, and turn it over to the cool side. Take some time to help someone, but remember: everyone is really out to get you.

June

~ Aries
Find a new use for duct tape. Your friends are beginning to suspect your television is broken, and you don't really have a "goth TV" after all. For a week this month, you will have an urge to put cheese on everything.

~ Taurus
Luck is going your way this month. The stars say it's time to take a gamble, either with love or with the slot machines. You have a knack for attracting the strangest people; you should start asking yourself why.

~ Gemini
A small change to your eating schedule could make a world of difference in your health. Eliminating the purging after every meal would be a step in the right direction. You'll spend less on laundry, too.

~ Cancer
You have a tendency to be your own worst critic. Cut yourself some slack. Everybody makes mistakes when they distribute medication once in a while. Repeat this month's affirmation: Everything I do brings me aliveness and joy and one day closer to parole. Make an effort to at least look like you're interested in your partner's point of view.

~ Leo
A deep desire to make more of yourself blossoms on the 14th, right before the last welfare check arrives. It could be the incentive you need to make that one big change in your life. Try to spend it on something other than just beer.

~ Virgo
Conflicts abound at home. Just keep telling your significant other it's absolutely necessary for you to keep working late at the office every

night for that big project that's coming up, and to never mind the funky smells on your clothes all the time. What are you, on trial here?

~ Libra
Focus your Chi on balancing your checkbook. As much as you appreciate the help of others, there are some things you just want to do by yourself, such as that thing you do in the bathroom before bed every night. It's nobody's business if you think about movie stars when you do it, either.

~ Scorpio
Things aren't going too well for your mate or your partner or a neighbor or a co-worker or somebody you barely know. The voice of wisdom will speak to you from the mouth of a singing fish that hangs on your wall. The winds of change blow in your direction, smelling something like asparagus.

~ Sagittarius
A Taurus and a Capricorn are giving you some grief, bothering you about that thing with the Gemini, so you call on a Libra for advice. An Aries may be the answer to your problems. Or not. When asked, politely reply to the nice man with the gun that you would be more than happy to put on his lovely blindfold.

~ Capricorn
This would be a good month to change your underwear. Concentrate on making new friends right up until the 21st, when you'll need all the friends you can get. Opinions are strong this month, much like your breath.

~ Aquarius
Between the 20th and the 27th, strive to balance your time between work, home, and the strip club. Do something nice for somebody named Ted. Financial good luck comes with courage, superior know-how, and occasional insider trading.

~ Pisces
Take time to enjoy the simpler things in life, like protozoa. Some exciting new ideas will come to you the first half of the month, but be prepared when your dreams are shattered like the last ice of winter

under the unforgiving sun of the first day of spring. Getting drunk afterwards will help.

July

~ Aries
You will be haunted by visions of a bright, enchanted land where hamburgers and French fries happily sing and dance before being devoured by an evil clown. Use an anti-static sheet when you run the dryer. Try to have a good time between the 2nd and the 17th, because you'll need some good memories to help you feel better after what happens on the 18th, you poor bastard.

~ Taurus
The planets can't wait for the return of football season. Although situations can look out of control, and times can seem very tense and hectic this month, try to relax. It's nothing serious. The universe is just yanking your chain. The first days of the month will challenge the strong points of your character, if any.

~ Gemini
Unique new opportunities of unclear substance will bring pleasant but vague surprises. You will take a walk near water either during the day or night with someone that has a vowel in his or her name. Grass will grow. The sun will rise in the east. At some point this month, you will sleep.

~ Cancer
You will read something that will remind you of something completely different and unrelated, and you will spend an inordinate amount of time this month trying to figure out what it was about the former that reminded you of the latter, exploring all options, at last coming to the conclusion you must be nuts. When invited to appear as a guest on a daytime talk show alongside all your former intimate partners, give it a pass.

~ Leo
Before taking on any new commitments, ask yourself some important questions, like: How did I get into this mess? Could I make it to the tree line before anyone notices? How good is their aim? In regards to that

special thing you do so well with your mouth: if your partner hesitates at French-kissing you immediately afterwards, it's nothing personal.

~ Virgo
When choosing a wine to serve with dinner, choose the one whose color matches your carpet. Don't let the fancy-pants food critics make you think they're not all the same. Besides, if good taste was an important part of your life, you'd be in big trouble. Express your individuality by wearing the exact same clothes as everyone else.

~ Libra
Routine tedious work can get boring sometimes, but you find ways to be creative and make work fun, such as mooning the people in the next building. This month, prepare for new surroundings and update your resume. Someone you used to be very close to will make a disturbing call to you from the free clinic.

~ Scorpio
Jupiter is tertiary, yet flaccid. A gathering of friends is in order this month. Alcoholic beverages should be in ample supply. Suggest a simple game of chance, and then take them to the cleaners. Synchronize your spirit with the sounds of the '70's in this great collection of hits, performed by their original artists.

~ Sagittarius
Neptune and Mercury move into separate quarters. A tender, intimate moment with a loved one will be made even more memorable with the presence of a hidden video camera. No matter how priceless the vintage, one thing is certain: after ten bottles, "taste" is really kind of a moot point.

~ Capricorn
Harm none with bright blessings when you merry meet your magical goddess, blessed be! Life can be confusing, and even more so for you. To reduce stress, have your home address tattooed on your hand. Repeat this month's affirmation: My light body is awakening and applying for a credit card.

~ Aquarius

Neither Venus nor Uranus invites Pluto to their parties. Events at home take center stage, or in the case of your family, center ring. The laughter and joy of family members brings much happiness until you realize they bought that new entertainment center with your credit card.

~ Pisces

What was it, exactly, that made Fonzie on "Happy Days" so popular? Was it the clothes? The hair? The motorcycle? No, it was the attitude. The independent spirit that burns inside of each of us, yearning to be free. Okay, and maybe the bike.

August

~ Aries

As the Moon travels from one house to the next, you wonder why it never pays rent. Someone that's either a friend or a stranger may or may not say something to you this month that will either make you feel better or not. If you were really in touch with yourself, you'd make yourself take showers more often.

~ Taurus

To have friends, you need to be a friend, or at least be able to afford to pay people to stand around and look like they're your friends. Spend a week sorting your socks. Repeat this month's affirmation: My cells and atoms are growing more radiant every day I live near the nuclear power plant.

~ Gemini

You will find yourself channeling the spiritual energy of a 10,000-old warrior from the lost continent of Atlantis who was never really that much fun to begin with. Spend some time hiding the cutlery, and ignore the urge to disembowel your enemies.

~ Cancer

Few events in your life, you will discover, adequately prepare you for prison. Your holistic cathartic aura is interrupted by a cosmic planetary alignment, causing a flux in the awakening of your synergistic transformational healing power. Re-attune your energy field with a generous helping of chocolate.

~ Leo
Angry emotions, moodiness and irritability are possible. The likely cause? Secret government satellites. Carry $20 in spare change with you at all times to confuse the orbiting magnetic sensors.

~ Virgo
Suppress the desire to share your thoughts on the political ramifications of environment irresponsibility on the ecosystems of South America. Between the 12th and the 17th, strive to get your trash out to the curb in time.

~ Libra
Exciting events are happening in your life. You are a clever, resourceful person, and hopefully that will be enough to help you survive being stranded in the desert for a week.

~ Scorpio
Disturbing news will come your way, but your spirits will rise when you figure out how to make a buck off it. If someone is going to profit from personal tragedy, why not you? Hold out for the highest bidder.

~ Sagittarius
The constellations in your third house keep wondering why they can't get basic cable TV. The first half of the month proves to be challenging up until you figure out how to open the garage door. On/off switches can be tricky sometimes.

~ Capricorn
Do your best at work, and chances are the girl with the big gazongas will still get the promotion. That's the universe's way of sticking it to you. Have patience, and trust in the healing wisdom of cheese. Some wonderful parting gifts await you.

~ Aquarius
This is the month to be helpful and understanding. Take time to encourage an open discussion of personal feelings between your family members, and be prepared for the fistfights that immediately follow. That personal relationship you've been dreaming about will only come true if the other five people are as willing as you are.

~ Pisces
Avoid overspending. Make a budget for the important things in your life, such as paperback books, condoms, and cable TV, and stick to it. Don't do that thing you were going to do, because if you do it, you're regret doing it much more than you'll regret not doing it. Someone close to you will show their true colors: blue and green.

September

~ Aries
The changes in your life continue. You'll find that cardboard can be surprisingly comfortable to sleep on, as compared to concrete. A new taste sensation will appear in the dumpster. Be prepared to defend your end of the bridge overpass.

~ Taurus
The planet Venus influences you to shop for a new couch. Your harmonious attunement with the ever-changing holistic universe will be a contributing factor when you easily find the TV remote. Success comes with a price: $17.56.

~ Gemini
Try to remember that the main characteristic of connection-oriented communication is that it provides assurance of packet delivery. Conflicts will arise when friends are unable to understand the special relationship you have with a particular lap-dancer. Don't listen to them. Follow your heart, and keep lots of dollar bills in your pockets.

~ Cancer
To touch is to feel. To feel is to know. To know is to take advantage of that special half-price offer, while supplies last. This month, maintain decorum, and behave like a perfect lady or gentleman, depending on which outfit you happen to be wearing at the time.

~ Leo
Take something you've had for a long time and give it to somebody you haven't given anything to for a long time because you'd meant to give them something on that special occasion but it kept slipping your mind and you thought you'd wait until a holiday or a weekend or something but don't— do it now.

~ Virgo
The weight you feel within you isn't guilt; it's the six boxes of Grape Nuts you had for breakfast. With Mercury in its current position, tactful communication is very important, and ARE YOU PAYING ATTENTION ?!?

~ Libra
Through hypnosis, it may distress you to research your past lives and discover you spent 600 generations reincarnating over and over as mold. Your world is expanding, much like your waistline. Remember: you are a decent person, no matter what your boss says about you. Or your co-workers. Or you friends and family and neighbors and former classmates.

~ Scorpio
Dangerous people you've never met are in the process of formulating life-altering events which you cannot even begin to understand in forbidden places you've never heard of. Try to not worry too much about it.

~ Sagittarius
There comes a point in everyone's life when they have to make a conscious decision: how much public embarrassment am I willing to live with? What's surprising is the number of times you will ask yourself that question this month.

~ Capricorn
You have a taste for drama, but be careful. A passionate outburst could ruin a delicate situation, so before making your feelings known, wait until you get out of the elevator. Try a little hydrocortisone on those rug burns.

~ Aquarius
Buy something expensive on the 6th, give up trying to make it work on the 9th, then take it back to the store on the 10th and get a replacement. Remember that early withdrawal may result in penalties. You need to synchronize transpersonal relationships with your spiritually cleansing energy fields, whatever the hell that means.

~ Pisces

There will be some intense chemistry with someone you had previously only thought of as the kind of friend you could borrow money from. It could blossom into something sticky. Repeat this month's affirmation: I expand myself and my cable service to my higher being.

October

~ Aries
Karma works. You sew what you reap. What goes around comes around. You get what you pay for. This month, be prepared to get everything you've got coming to you. While there's still time, make sure your insurance is up to date.

~ Taurus
The New Moon will bring a heightened sense of touch, and woolen clothes will seem much itchier. By the 20th, try to get TV cable service restored. You only hurt the ones you love to hurt.

~ Gemini
Your most significant aspect this month is your ability to communicate, so now would be a good time to tell your intimate partner about the "happy toys" under the bed. Have faith in your dreams, including the one where you're dressed up like Carmen Miranda.

~ Cancer
Your long-held assumption that the world is secret run by chipmunks will be called into question. You will be visited by a number of close, personal friends who like to periodically drop by, eat all your food, use up all your hot water, drink all your booze, and then leave. No matter what happens on the 3rd, be strong, and hope the swelling goes down soon.

~ Leo
Be all that you could be if you could be anything you wanted to be when you dreamed about what you could be. Be sure to be that which you wish to be. Beware the bees!

~ Virgo
Some people just aren't as open-minded as you when it comes to personal hygiene. A sudden desire to contact a far-away friend will

ultimately result in unexpected roaming charges. It would be unlikely anyone could think less of you.

~ Libra
Saturn turns to Mars for some financial advice. A close friend has a body part nicknamed "Goliath." This month you could be surrounded by many social activities. Somebody could actually think of you when they plan their event, and, as crazy as it sounds, indeed be happy if you attend. It could happen.

~ Scorpio
You have a lot to learn when it comes to commitment. For that matter, you have a lot to learn about geography, calculus, and the effects of the Industrial Revolution on western class structure. Be ready for a pop quiz. Very soon, you will find out that being on national TV isn't as much fun as you thought it would be.

~ Sagittarius
Events happen quickly. Pay attention. You will regret it if you let an amazing opportunity slip by you just because you were busy doing something futile and meaningless, like reading predictions of your future. Repeat this month's affirmation: I bring the angelic kingdom into my life through telemarketing techniques.

~ Capricorn
Now that you have little time to do it, the thing you should have done when you had plenty of time to do it still needs to be done. This is a month of self-evaluation, a period when you look at yourself much more than you already do. Take a moment to ponder why you have so many mirrors and photos of yourself in your house. Consider getting more.

~ Aquarius
The planet Jupiter influences you to wash your car. In a moment of introspection, you'll come to a simple and logical conclusion about the state of human existence but it will be so obvious that you'll feel like a total dweeb for not seeing it before and immediately forget it. When your co-workers say they're not laughing at you they're laughing with you, they're lying.

~ Pisces
Mars conjoins with Uranus for a potluck dinner. For a brief moment this month, it will really suck to be you. One particular issue you've been dealing with has been a major personal problem for you, mostly because discovering a workable resolution would involve logic and reason; you need to find what works best for you.

November

~ Aries
Your bashful attitude will be because your doc prescribed some dopey pills for you sneezy allergies, which made you grumpy and sleepy, but rest assured that when the pills wear off, you will be happy again.

~ Taurus
The temptation to photograph one of your body parts is great, but resist it, regardless of how proud of it you might be. Just remember last time hoo, boy! Repeat this month's affirmation: I am working up to a quantum leap of faith with little baby steps.

~ Gemini
If you have experienced hair loss, nausea and skin rashes after traveling too close to a mysterious black truck westbound on Interstate 40 recently, it's probably nothing. A special someone really likes it when you do that thing with your tongue, you know, that thing where you turn it so it feels kind of like it does when you move your head that certain way? Ooooh.

~ Cancer
Things look bad on the 2nd, but get better by the 9th, and although someone may say something scary on the 11th, it doesn't mean the situation will not resolve itself by the 16th, leading you to have some fun on the 19th with someone who will tell you on the 28th that you need to see a doctor immediately.

~ Leo
Economic indicators may help you determine the overall outlook for the economy and possibly your personal portfolio. Or something like that. It's a tough call. A lot of this predicting stuff is just one big crap shoot, when you get down to it.

~ Virgo

Venus just isn't in the mood. Life can sometimes seem like an old vinyl record that's been left out in the sun to melt into the shape of a buttercup. Your reputation will be in need of an overhaul this month, especially after what happens with the sheep. Refrigerate your ketchup, to keep it fresh. Try to be smarter.

~ Libra

When faced with the choice between humiliation and guilt, be sure you make the right decision. With you, either works equally well. Ignore the laughter of others every time you walk by.

~ Scorpio

Mercury and Saturn glare at each other. The cycle of life is complex, yet simple. We are born, we live, we watch TV, and then we die... But, when you get down to it, does any of us really, really "watch" TV? You may experience some discomfort.

~ Sagittarius

The first part of the month swings around and whomps you upside the head, but after that things will go much easier in your life. It's all a matter of perspective. Channel the hidden powers of your inner aura into something that might actually make some money for a change. The change of seasons prompts you to change your sheets.

~ Capricorn

Events are happening fast in your professional life, but if you hurry you'll still have time to shred all the incriminating evidence. Remember: it's all about you. Now would be a good time to start developing a taste for jailhouse food.

~ Aquarius

Neptune and the Sun have issues. Trying your best might not get you what you want, but you can rest assured everyone around you will get a good laugh out of it. Failure can be funny. Be satisfied your friends are so entertained.

~ Pisces

Horoscope? Yeah, we got your horoscope. We got it right HERE, pal! Relationships are very important. Friends and partners need to know how you feel so that they can properly relate with you. If you make your case and they still do not understand the person you really are, well then, the hell with them.

December

~ Aries
Communication with your partner needs some improvement. It would make the home situation better to live with. You need to sit down together and talk about your interests, your common goals, and why it's still necessary for you to walk five steps behind your partner in public.

~ Taurus
It's okay to make people feel bad to get sympathy. For you, it works. You will be blessed by dreams of the mighty Hamster God, and visions of the Great Habbitrail in the Sky.

~ Gemini
Wear more plaid. Don't think of yourself as predictable, as being in a rut, or being too pathetically timid to make any kind of change in the repetitive, nonstop assembly line of your life. Think of yourself as "dependable," and get back to work.

~ Cancer
Awaiting the decision of the judges, Pluto and the Moon return to their respective corners. Something you did a couple of months ago someplace where you usually go will finally take effect, and the results will be overwhelmingly obvious, unless you forgot what it was you did in the first place. Think more.

~ Leo
Romance will return this month for someone close to you, who will brag about his intimate moments over and over in graphic detail. You will eventually get really sick of it, and relate a graphic story of your own about their romantic partner and a local college hockey team. Life is good.

~ Virgo

That little act you do where you look like you never know what's going on and you're confused about life in general was starting to get old with your friends, until they realized it wasn't an act. Pet more dogs.

~ Libra
The next full moon will either stir up some long-forgotten memories, or transform you into a horrible, man-eating werewolf. It's a tough call. Don't be surprised this month if meet someone new and get kissed some place you've never been kissed before. You might even enjoy it. Try not to yodel too much.

~ Scorpio
Your reincarnated personal growth crystals are trying to tell you that your inner karmic consciousness is awakening to a new level of energy, a state of being in which you will never have a problem parallel parking your car. Happiness is almost within throwing distance.

~ Sagittarius
Think of everything you have to feel guilty about in your life as big, heavy rocks. All of these rocks are in a backpack you carry with you all the time. Now imagine you're climbing Mt. Everest with this huge backpack of rocks on your back. That pretty much sums up your life this month.

~ Capricorn
A close acquaintance is pressuring you to invest in their latest get- rich-quick schemed, but you're not falling for that line again. Don't give in to intimidation; if you want to lose your shirt again, let it be your decision. Try to spit farther.

~ Aquarius
Weekends this month will be filled with fun and excitement, danger and romance, mystery and thrills, at least until the half-off coupons from the video rental store run out. Repeat this month's affirmation: I follow my inner guidance with action, and the advice of the voices in my head with caution.

~ Pisces

The Necronomicrap

Despite all the troubles and tribulations people go through in their everyday lives, you can always count on the sunrise bringing a whole new day to deal with the problems. Or, to put it another way, don't do today what you can put off until tomorrow. You'll be glad you did.

Tim Frayser

One Final Note...

The point of astrology is that objects in space have influence over your life. However, most astrologers forget about one overwhelmingly influential object: the Earth! Hey, the Earth is an object in space, isn't it? It's that big thing under your feet. The Earth, just by its proximity, pretty much has veto power over all the other astronomical influences. In the area of astrology, two schools of thought have developed.

There are those who discount and ignore the influence of the Earth altogether, and focus completely on the non-Earth objects and their powers over human existence. When things go wrong, this point of view makes it easy to blame anything and anybody other than ourselves for our subsequent unhappiness. Then, there are those that accept the presence of the Earth, embracing the idea that humans, not the stars, wield complete power over human destiny. Whichever view one takes, people should take a moment to examine that view of astrology indeed, of life itself and reflect on how that view makes one a better person. The latter viewpoint may not be as pretty or as romantic as the former one, but a mature, responsible world still has plenty of room for beauty and romance.

The radical idea that each of us is ultimately responsible for our own happiness may not be received well by some, but it may be an idea people of the 21st century are finally evolved enough to accept.

... Evolution... Hmmm, that might be a good subject for a book...

Tim Frayser

About the Author

Tim Frayser has been telling stories since he first learned to talk. A past vice president of the Oklahoma Collegiate Press Association, he holds a bachelor's degree in journalism from Northeastern State University in Tahlequah, Oklahoma.

Tim has been active in science fiction fandom for over twenty-five years. He is a former chairman of the Conestoga science fiction convention in Tulsa, was a guest at Czarkon 12, and has shown his cartoon art in various Midwest art shows. For three years, he was editorial cartoonist for a weekly independent newspaper in Tulsa. He frequently writes grouchy letters to the editor.

Tim currently works for the City of Tulsa as a computer support analyst. He is also a photographer, third-degree black belt, Star Trek fan, amateur documentary film maker, Civil War buff, and ordained minister. His likes are backrubs, talking with friends, and long walks on the beach. He lives in Broken Arrow, Oklahoma, with his wife, three children, a dog and a psychotic cat.

Tim Frayser

About the Artist

Mike Cole has been a fan of science fiction since the early 70's when they began to run STAR TREK in syndication. Comic books and other TV shows of the era followed and slowly began to rot Mike's mind from the inside out, at least according to his parents.

In the 80's Mike discovered science fiction conventions and realized that there were other people in the world just as weird as him. After a tour of duty in the Marine Corp (yes, I know what you're thinking, Mike was a Marine?! *Yeeesh!*) he was able to pursue art on a more dedicated basis and began to display his artwork and cartoons in shows and auctions all over the country.

Mike lives in St. Charles, Missouri, where the unsuspecting citizens think he is a quiet, unassuming young man who keeps to himself, but by night he becomes the masked avenger…

CARTOOOON FANBOOOOY!!!

Tim Frayser

Yard Dog Press Titles as Of This Print Date

A Bubba in Time Saves None, Edited by Selina Rosen
A Man, A Plan, (yet lacking) A Canal, Panama, Linda Donahue
Adventures of the Irish Ninja, Selina Rosen
The Alamo and Zombies, Jean Stuntz
All the Marbles, Dusty Rainbolt
Almost Human, Gary Moreau
Ancient Enemy, Lee Killough
Angels of Mercy, Laura J. Underwood
Another Breath, Gary Moreau
The Anthology From Hell: Humorous Tales From WAY Down Under,
    Edited by Julia S. Mandala
Ard Magister, Laura J. Underwood
Assassins Inc., Phillip Drayer Duncan
Assassins Incorporated: Rehired, Phillip Drayer Duncan
Bad City, Selina Rosen & Laura J. Underwood
Bad Lands, Selina Rosen & Laura J. Underwood
Black Rage, Selina Rosen
Blackrose Avenue, Mark Shepherd
The Boat Man, Selina Rosen
Bobby's Troll, John Lance
Bride of Tranquility, Tracy S. Morris
Bruce and Roxanne from Start to Finnish, Rie Sheridan Rose
The Bubba Chronicles, Selina Rosen
Bubba Fables, Sue P. Sinor
Bubbas Of the Apocalypse, Edited by Selina Rosen
The Burden of the Crown, Selina Rosen
Chains of Redemption, Selina Rosen
Checking On Culture, Lee Killough
Chronicles of the Last War, Laura J. Underwood
Dadgum Martians Invade the Lucky Nickel Saloon, Ken Rand
Dark and Stormy Nights, Bradley H. Sinor
Deja Doo, Edited by Selina Rosen
Dracula's Lawyer, Julia S. Mandala
Dragon's Tongue, Laura J. Underwood
Escape Velocities, Brian A. Hopkins
The Essence of Stone, Beverly A. Hale
Fairy BrewHaHa at the Lucky Nickel Saloon, Ken Rand
The Fantastikon: Tales of Wonder, Robin Wayne Bailey
Fire & Ice, Selina Rosen
Flush Fiction, Volume I: Stories To Be Read In One Sitting, Edited by

The Necronomicrap

Playing With Secrets, Bradley H & Sue P. Sinor
Redheads In Love, Linda L. Donahue, Rhonda Eudaly, Julia S.
    Mandala, & Dusty Rainbolt
Reruns, Selina Rosen
Rock 'n' Roll Universe, Ken Rand
Shadows In Green, Richard Dansky
Stories That Won't Make Your Parents Hurl, Edited by Selina Rosen
Strange Robby, Selina Rosen
Tales from Keltora, Laura J. Underwood
*Tales of the Lucky Nickel Saloon, Second Ave., Laramie, Wyoming, U S
    of A,* Ken Rand
Tarbox Station, Rhonda Eudaly
Texistani: Indo-Pak Food from a Texas Kitchen, Beverly A. Hale
That's All Folks, J. F. Gonzalez
Through Wyoming Eyes, Ken Rand
Tranquility, Tracy Morris
Turn Left to Tomorrow, Robin Wayne Bailey
The Twins, Selina Rosen
The Undead At My Head, Ethan Nahté
Villains in Training, Julia S. Mandala and Linda L. Donahue
Wandering Lark, Laura J. Underwood
Weirdough, Inc., Selina Rosen and Sherri Dean
Wings of Morning, Katharine Eliska Kimbriel
Zombies in Oz and Other Undead Musings, Robin Wayne Bailey

Fantasy Writers Asylum (A YDP Imprint):

Blood Songs, Julia Mandala
Chaos Heir: Beholden A. D. Guzman
Death's Paladin Christopher Donahue
Gateway to Corimar, Julia Mandala & Linda L. Donahue
Spirit Poles, Julia Mandala & Linda L. Donahue
Tale of the Black Heart, Linda L. Donahue
Traitor's Gate, Linda L. Donahue & Julia Mandala

Double Dog (A YDP Imprint):

#1:
Of Stars & Shadows, Mark W. Tiedemann
This Instance Of Me, Jeffrey Turner

#2: *Out of print*
Gods and Other Children, Bill D. Allen
Tranquility, Tracy Morris

#3:
Home Is the Hunter, James K. Burk
Farstep Station, Lazette Gifford

#4:
Sabre Dance, Melanie Fletcher
The Lunari Mask, Laura J. Underwood

#5:
House of Doors, Julia Mandala
Jaguar Moon, Linda A. Donahue

Just Cause (A YDP Imprint):

The Bitter End, Selina Rosen
Death Under the Crescent Moon, Dusty Rainbolt
Duckrt: Mystery at the Museum, Zeb Rosenzweig
Duckrt Escapes from Jail, Zeb Rosenzweig
Duckrt The Lost Story, Zeb Rosenzweig
Getting It Real, Selina Rosen
The Ghost Writer, Selina Rosen
It's Not Rocket Science: Spirituality for the Working-Class Soul, Selina Rosen
Meditations of a Hoarder, Melinda LaFevers
Not My Life, Selina Rosen
Permanent Solution to a Temporary Problem, Selina Rosen
The Pit, Selina Rosen
Plots and Protagonists: A Reference Guide for Writers, Mel. White
Vanishing Fame, Selina Rosen
Why I Blame Trump on Jesus and Other Things I Don't Dare Say Out Loud Selina Rosen
Yard Dog Color the Covers Coloring Book Brad Foster

www.ingramcontent.com/pod-product-compliance
Lightning Source LLC
Chambersburg PA
CBHW030518130626
46549CB00007B/3048